Dear Parents:

Congratulations! Your child is taking the first steps on an exciting journey. The destination? Independent reading!

STEP INTO READING® will help your child get there. The program offers five steps to reading success. Each step includes fun stories and colorful art or photographs. In addition to original fiction and books with favorite characters, there are Step into Reading Non-Fiction Readers, Phonics Readers and Boxed Sets, Sticker Readers, and Comic Readers—a complete literacy program with something to interest every child.

Learning to Read, Step by Step!

Ready to Read   Preschool–Kindergarten
• big type and easy words • rhyme and rhythm • picture clues
For children who know the alphabet and are eager to begin reading.

Reading with Help   Preschool–Grade 1
• basic vocabulary • short sentences • simple stories
For children who recognize familiar words and sound out new words with help.

Reading on Your Own   Grades 1–3
• engaging characters • easy-to-follow plots • popular topics
For children who are ready to read on their own.

Reading Paragraphs   Grades 2–3
• challenging vocabulary • short paragraphs • exciting stories
For newly independent readers who read simple sentences with confidence.

Ready for Chapters   Grades 2–4
• chapters • longer paragraphs • full-color art
For children who want to take the plunge into chapter books but still like colorful pictures.

STEP INTO READING® is designed to give every child a successful reading experience. The grade levels are only guides; children will progress through the steps at their own speed, developing confidence in their reading.

Remember, a lifetime love of reading starts with a single step!

Visit us on the Web!
StepIntoReading.com
rhcbooks.com

ISBN 978-0-525-64731-7 (trade) — ISBN 978-0-525-64732-4 (lib. bdg.)

Printed in the United States of America

10 9 8 7 6 5 4 3 2 1

nick jr.™

nick jr.
Nella
THE PRINCESS KNIGHT

THE SHARE FAIR

adapted from the teleplay "The Share Faire"
by Liam Farrell

by Delphine Finnegan

illustrated by Nneka Myers

Random House 🏠 New York

There was a craft fair
at Princess Nella's
school one day.

Everyone made crafts
to share.

Princess Nella and
Trinket made tiaras.
They used beautiful
flowers.

The two friends
could not wait
to share their tiaras!

7

Sir Garrett and Clod
made funny
sock puppets.

Willow and Minatori
made yummy
lemonade.

Everyone wanted

Nella and Trinket's tiaras!

Sir Blaine was not happy.

No one wanted

his balloon swords.

Sir Blaine snuck behind
Nella and Trinket's stand.
He knocked dirt
all over their flowers.

Oh, no!
The dirt flattened
the flowers.

Nella cleaned off
the flowers.
She had an idea.

She made necklaces
with the flat flowers.
Everybody wanted one!

Sir Blaine had
a new plan.
He stretched a balloon
to fling the flowers away!

Nella and Trinket

caught the flowers!

But all the petals fell off.

Nella made bracelets
from the stems!

Next, Sir Blaine
took Willow's
magic plant food.
He made a giant plant.

The giant plant
grabbed Sir Blaine!

Nella knew what to do.

She turned into

a Princess Knight!

Nella used Sir Blaine's balloons to rescue him.

The fair was saved.

Everyone cheered!

Sir Blaine thanked Nella
with a balloon tiara
and sword.